Earth
Daughter

Alicia of Ácoma Pueblo

by George Ancona

Simon & Schuster Books for Young Readers

To the people who made this book possible: Jackie Shutiva Histia and
Bennett Greg Histia for welcoming me into their lives; Reginal Pasqual,
the governor of Ácoma Pueblo, for his encouragement; Alana McGrattan,
librarian at the Santa Fe Indian School, for introducing me to the
Histia family; Louise Stiver of the Museum of Indian Arts and
Culture, for her help and cooperation in photographing the
Ácoma pottery in the collection; David Grant Noble and
John Garrigan, for sharing their knowledge and
experience. My thanks to you all.

SIMON & SCHUSTER BOOKS FOR YOUNG READERS
An imprint of Simon & Schuster Children's Publishing Division
1230 Avenue of the Americas, New York, New York 10020

SIMON & SCHUSTER BOOKS FOR YOUNG READERS is a trademark
of Simon & Schuster.

Book design by George Ancona
The text of this book is set in 13 point ITC Weidemann.
Manufactured in the United States of America
First edition
10 9 8 7 6 5 4 3 2 1
Library of Congress Cataloging-in-Publication Data
Ancona, George.
Earth daughter : Alicia of Ácoma Pueblo / George Ancona. — 1st ed.
   p.   cm.
ISBN 0-689-80322-2
1. Histia, Alicia—Juvenile literature. 2. Ácoma Indians—Biography—
Juvenile literature. 3. Ácoma Indians—Juvenile literature.
[1. Ácoma Indians. 2. Indians of North America. 3. Pottery craft. 4. Histia, Alicia.] I. Title.
E99.A16H573   1995   978.9'91004974—dc20
[B]   94-48252

Courtesy of the Museum of Indian Arts and Culture / Laboratory of
Anthology, Ácoma jar with bird motif, Circa 1900–1920, #35748/12,
Ácoma jar with intricate geometric designs, 1951, Eva Vallo or
Mary Histia, Ácoma Seed Jar, 1987, Gilbert Chino.

*Á*coma was built a thousand years ago on top of a magnificent 360-foot-high *mesa* in New Mexico. When the Spanish came to the Southwest in the sixteenth century, they called the clusters of *adobe* buildings they saw *pueblo,* the Spanish word for "town." The native people who live in pueblos came to be known as *Pueblo* Indians. There are nineteen pueblos built along the Rio Grande.

Some people believe Ácoma is the oldest continuously inhabited pueblo in the United States. Today only a few families live in the pueblo. Most of the people live in small settlements around the mesa. But they still consider the pueblo a sacred place, and they gather there for their traditional ceremonies and dances.

Alicia lives in one of the nearby communities, but her family still has a house in the pueblo, where they gather on feast days and holidays. Ácoma potters are known for their beautiful ceramics. Visitors to the pueblo have a chance to buy a pot directly from its maker. "When I grow up, I want to be a potter and also go to college to become a lawyer," says Alicia.

But for now Alicia loves giggling with her friends in the playground and running with the cross-country team. "I like to compete because we get to go away and see places I've never been to." After school, Alicia likes collecting stamps and playing with her cousin and her little sister, Lindsay.

Alicia's older brother, Jonathan, and her sister Shelley spend school days away at the Indian High School in Santa Fe. On weekends the entire family is together. Alicia, Shelley, and Lindsay help their mother cook and make *tortillas*.

Like many of the people of Ácoma, Alicia's parents are potters. Her mother, Jackie Shutiva, makes *pinch pots*. Her dad, Greg Histia, makes pots with traditional Pueblo designs.

Pueblo people believe that they came up from the earth. So when a Pueblo potter gathers clay and works it into a beautiful pot, it expresses the people's closeness to their land—Mother Earth.

"Pinch pots were used for cooking," says Jackie, "because they heat up quickly. The many dips around the pot transfer the heat to the food faster than a smooth-sided one." Jackie was taught to make pots by her mother. Now Jackie teaches Alicia and Lindsay the same way her mother taught her.

Alicia and her parents begin by searching for the clay they need among the canyons. When they find a dry clay deposit, they pray before digging. "It's our way of giving thanks to Mother Earth for sharing her clay with us," explains Jackie. "It gives life to the pottery, helps us find new shapes and designs, and hope that there will be more clay when we come back."

Dry clay is hard and lumpy. Jackie soaks it in water for a few days to soften it and breaks the lumps with her hands.

On a morning when Alicia is in school, Jackie and Lindsay search the ruins of a house for *shards* of broken pots. She grinds the shards on a stone called a *metate*. This is the *temper* that is mixed with the clay to keep the pots from cracking when they are dried and fired.

Alicia and Jackie then knead the clay while adding the temper to it until it is smooth. "Some people mix clay with their feet," says Jackie, "but I have more strength in my arms so I do it this way." Working with clay is a slow process. It cannot be rushed; clay doesn't want you to be angry with it.

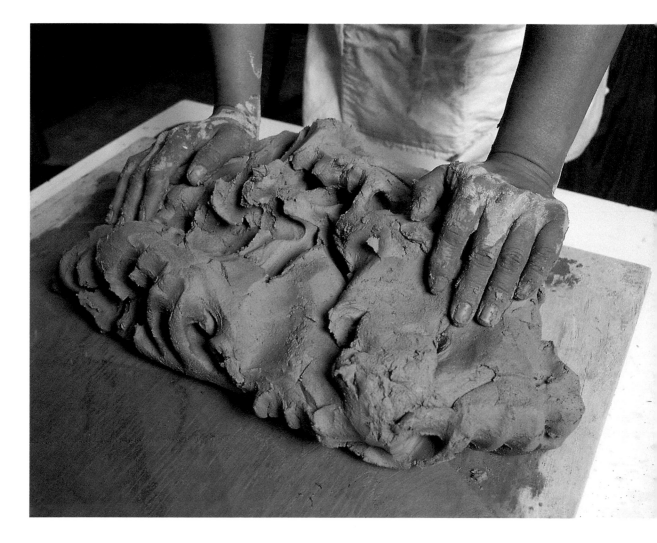

When the clay is well mixed, Jackie wraps it in a wet cloth to keep it moist for the day they use it. But now they have to prepare for the coming feast day.

Each pueblo has a feast day to celebrate its patron saint. In addition to the dances, there are races and lots of eating. So the days before a feast day are a time for cooking and baking.

With hugs, kisses, and tickles, the family gathers at Alicia's grandparents' house, where a hot fire is made in the *horno,* the outdoor oven. In the kitchen Alicia works with her grandmother, forming loaves and rolls of bread dough.

Chili stew, *tamales,* oven bread, and *fry bread* feed the family and guests that come from far away. On feast days friends, and sometimes even strangers, are invited into pueblo homes to eat. "My mother told me never to count how much food there is or for sure you will run out," says Jackie. "If you don't count, you never run out."

When the fire dies down in the horno, Alicia's uncle sweeps out the ashes and her grandmother fills the hot oven with the bread. Then she covers the opening and everyone goes on to do other chores. It is dark by the time Alicia's grandmother uncovers the horno and takes out the hot golden-colored loaves of bread. Of course, Alicia and Lindsay sample the first warm buns, and then it's home and off to bed.

After school, Alicia works with her mother. She makes little clay hornos and turtles, but she likes making little snakes the best. "Me and my brother once found a snake. It was bluish and shiny. I stood right in front of it and it didn't do anything to me. That's why I like to make them," Alicia explains.

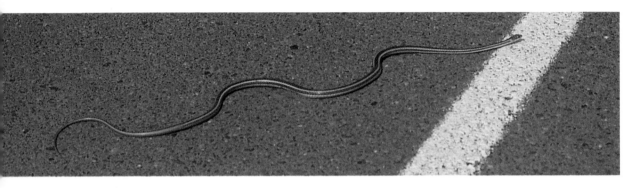

"I don't like snakes," says Jackie, "but I never run over them when I see them on the road. The old folks say that if you do, next morning you will have a flat tire."

After Alicia makes a few snakes, Jackie shows her how to form the base for a pot. To make a smooth-sided pot, Alicia rolls out a heavy coil of clay, flattens it, and attaches it to the base. Then she adds more flat coils to build up the sides of the pot. Each layer is blended into the previous one with a *gourd* or a stick so that the sides become a solid, smooth surface.

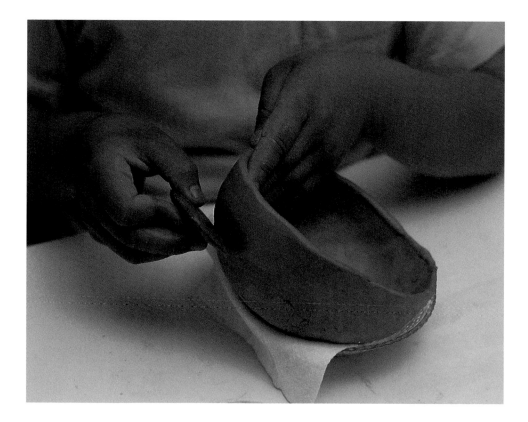

Across the table Jackie builds up her pinch pot with thin coils. Then she makes impressions along the coil with a stick or by pinching the clay with her fingers. This is why they are called pinch pots. "It gives me a wonderful feeling," says Jackie, "when I look at the shard of an old pinch pot and see the fingerprints of the person who made it hundreds of years ago." Jackie finishes the pot with a snake's head on the end of the last coil.

When the pots and snakes, turtles, and little hornos are dry, it is
time to decorate them. Jackie finds a *yucca* plant and cuts off a few
leaves. At home she cuts them into shorter pieces, which she chews
to separate the strands of fiber into a brush. Alicia tries to make a
brush, too. "Ugh, it tastes gross," says Alicia, and she uses a store-
bought brush instead.

The black color is made by rubbing a black stone on a rock *mortar* and mixing it with water. After the designs are painted, the pots are ready for firing. But pots can only be fired on a clear, dry, and windless day, so they must wait for such a day to come.

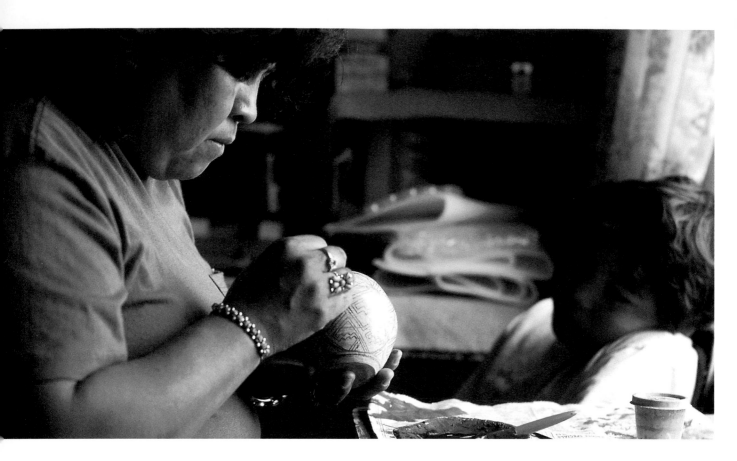

While they wait, Alicia visits her neighbor, Harriet Garcia. Mrs. Garcia lives next door to Alicia's pueblo home. Alicia watches Mrs. Garcia decorate seed pots. Ácoma pottery is known for its unique designs. The designs include deer, rain, lightning, corn, birds, and symbols from Pueblo myths and legends.

Mrs. Garcia tells Alicia the story of the *Kokopeli*. "He was a mythical character," says Mrs. Garcia, "who was hired by the people of the mesa to rid the pueblo of lizards and ants. After he did so, the people of the pueblo refused to give him the promised fee. So he played his flute and all the children followed him to a huge cottonwood tree. He would pull down a branch for the children to grab and then he let it go. The branch sprung up and hurled the children into the sky, where they turned into blackbirds."

At last, a clear, dry, and windless day arrives. Jackie makes a circle of stones and fills it with the dry cow manure that she and the children have gathered for the firing. She puts large pieces of shards on the manure and places the pottery to be fired on them. Then she covers them with more shards and manure. Finally she tucks kindling and newspapers around the mound of manure and lights it. The flames leap up and spread, burning with a hot, fiery intensity.

When the fire dies down, Jackie brushes the ashes and shards aside, revealing the hardened pottery. Some pieces have broken. They will be used as shards for future pots. Jackie is pleased with the results, and now her pots and Alicia's snakes, turtles, and hornos are ready for market.

Alicia likes to go with her parents to sell their work at the many craft fairs. She enters her work in the children's competitions and sometimes wins a prize. Alicia also sells her own snakes, pots, and turtles alongside her parents' pottery. The biggest fair is the annual Santa Fe Indian Market. People come from all over the world to buy pottery, crafts, and art.

Dancers from various pueblos perform at these fairs for the visitors
who come to shop.

Dances are a traditional ceremony for the Pueblo people. Since she was eight, Alicia has been dancing with her mother and sister. "I was so nervous the first time," she recalls, "but I just watched my mother's feet." All her dancing clothes, her *manta,* and her jewelry have been made or passed on to her by her relatives.

Dancing behind her mother and in front of her older sister, Alicia follows her mother's steps. Dust rises from the earth as the dancers' feet move to the rhythm of the drums. And so Alicia continues her pueblo's traditions, growing into her place among her people, her *clan,* and her family.

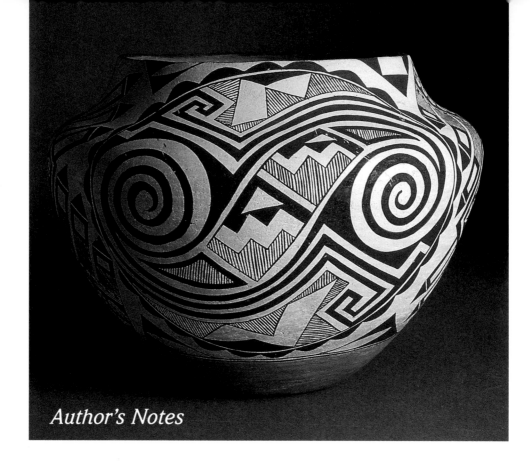

Alicia and her family are the direct descendants of the *Anasazi.* They are the first agricultural people who lived in the Southwest of what is now the United States, about two thousand years ago. They built towns and villages and developed the art of pottery making.

About one hundred miles northwest of Ácoma lie the Anasazi ruins of Chaco Canyon. Anasazi means "the ancient ones." Pottery shards excavated there include pinch pots like the ones that Jackie Shutiva makes. They used pots to serve, store, and cook food. Today, pottery has become an art form that expresses the Pueblo people's relationship to the earth and their culture.

The people of Ácoma speak *Keresan.* They affectionately call Ácoma "Ako," which in Keresan means "a place that always was." They also refer to the pueblo as Sky City. The Keres built Ácoma on top of the mesa to protect themselves from the marauding tribes that attacked them. In the plains below, they planted their crops. In order to get to the top, they had to climb, using toeholds and fingerholds along the face of the mesa. All the adobe bricks and *vigas* to build their houses had to be carried up to the mesa. The pueblo has been able to survive invasions and attacks by the Navajos, the Apaches, the Spanish, the Mexicans, and the Anglo-Americans who have come over the centuries. The Keres have always been in Ácoma and were never forced to relocate, like so many other Native American tribes.

When the Spanish *conquistadores* arrived in 1540, they brought with them missionaries who over the years tried to convert the Pueblo people to Roman Catholicism. The beautiful adobe church was built in the early 1600s. It is where traditional dances are performed to honor San Estevan, their patron saint, and to celebrate other holy days.

Today a road leads up to the mesa, enabling cars to drive up. A bus takes visitors up to the pueblo, where they can walk about, see the church, and shop for pottery. On certain ceremonial days the pueblo is closed to the public, but on other days visitors are welcome to watch the dancing.

Glossary

Ácoma—pueblo on a mesa in New Mexico

adobe—sun-dried clay brick

Anasazi—early settlers in the Southwest

clan—group of people of common descent; a family

conquistadores—Spanish soldiers that explored the Americas

fry bread—a biscuitlike bread made of wheat flour

gourd—fruit whose shell hardens when dry

horno—outdoor oven of stone and clay

Keresan—language spoken by six of the Rio Grande pueblos

Kokopeli—a figure from Pueblo mythology

manta—woman's dress made of black wool

mesa—land formation with a flat top and steep rock walls

metate—stone with a concave surface for grinding

mortar—bowl-shaped vessel

pinch pot—corrugated clay pot

pueblo—group of adobe houses

Pueblo—Native Americans belonging to one of the Rio Grande pueblos

shard—piece of broken pottery

tamale—cornmeal dough with a filling wrapped in corn husk

temper—substance added to clay to make it stronger

tortilla—thin, round pancake of cornmeal or wheat flour

viga—log used to support roof of adobe house

yucca—plant with stiff pointed leaves and white flowers

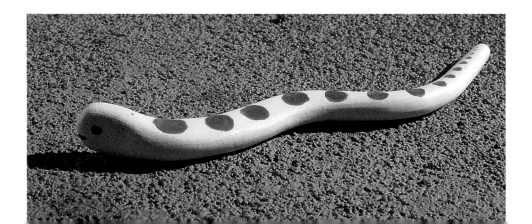